B

A. A. Livingston • Illustrated by Joey Chou

B. Bear and Lolly
Off to School

HARPER

An Imprint of HarperCollinsPublishers

To my own "baby bear." (And "husband bear," too!)
—A.A.L.

To my wonderful sister, Christine
—J.C.

B. Bear and Lolly: Off to School

Library of Congress Cataloging-in-Publication Data

Livingston, A. A.
 B. Bear and Lolly: off to school / A. A. Livingston ; illustrated by Joey Chou.
  p.   cm.
 Summary: B. Bear, formerly known as Baby Bear, from the classic story "Goldilocks and the Three Bears,"
realizes the importance of friendship when he and his best friend, Lolly, attend the first day of school.
 ISBN 978-0-06-219788-7 (trade bdg.) — ISBN 978-0-06-219789-4 (lib. bdg.)
 [1. First day of school—Fiction. 2. Friendship—Fiction. 3. Bears—Fiction. 4. Characters in literature—
Fiction.] I. Chou, Joey, ill. II. Title. III. Title: B. Bear and Lolly: off to school.
PZ7.L755Baam 2014   2012004290
[E]—dc23   CIP
                                                                                              AC

The artist used Adobe Illustrator to create the digital illustrations for this book. Typography by Martha Rago.
14 15 16 17 18 SCP 10 9 8 7 6 5 4 3 2 1
❖
First Edition

B.Bear and Lolly were the best of friends.
And why not? They liked the same porridge, the same
chair, and the same comfy bed.

They did all sorts of stuff together:

Skipping stones

Playing in the sand

Finding snacks

Looking at books

Creating masterpieces

Playing catch

As summer came to a close, B. Bear was thinking about the first day of school.

"Kindergarten starts next week!" he said. "I can't wait to do math and science and spelling and learn to read! What are you excited about, Lolly?"

She grinned. "I'm excited about recess!"

B. Bear laughed. "Oh, golly, Lolly!"

That afternoon, the friends decided to get everything they needed for school. They went to the woodcutter's store in the hollow of a tree.

Then it was time to pick out what to wear for their first day.

Too big. Too small.

Too hot. Too cold.

Too dark. Too bright.

Too silly!

Finally, they found outfits that were
JUST RIGHT!

On the first day of school, B. Bear and Lolly had breakfast together. Unfortunately, B. Bear was in a furry frenzy.

"Mama, what if no one likes me?" asked B. Bear.

"Oh, honey bear, what if *everyone* likes you?" Mama Bear said warmly.

Lolly agreed. "Besides, *I* like you," she said with a smile.

That made B. Bear smile, too.

Suddenly the cuckoo clock chirped.

"We can't be late on the first day!" B. Bear exclaimed.

He kissed his mama and papa good-bye, grabbed his backpack, and pulled Lolly out the door.

B. Bear ran down the forest path. "Hurry, Lolly! Hurry!"

"Don't worry—I know a shortcut," said Lolly.
She turned right at a craggy rock, hopped
over a mossy log, and passed by a house
made of straw.

"Are we there yet?" B. Bear groaned. "This backpack weighs a ton."

"Why did you bring so much stuff?" asked Lolly.

"I had to be prepared," B. Bear said. "What about you? Where's your stuff?"

"Right here," said Lolly, pulling a pencil from her hair. "But I may have packed too much."

The pair came to a tree that had
fallen across a stream.

"Now," said Lolly, "here's the tricky part."

"What? Convincing me to walk
over that?" asked B. Bear.

Lolly took a few steps across.
She turned and said,
"Come on, Ba—"

"Don't call me Baby!" B. Bear
exclaimed. "I'm a big bear."

B. Bear took a deep breath and
bravely walked forward. His claws
dug into the wet wood.

But Lolly didn't have claws.
She just had new shoes that were *verrrry* slippery.
B. Bear reached for his friend.

B. Bear swam over to her. "Lolly!
Lolly! Are you okay?"
"That was so much fun!" said
Lolly. "Let's do it again!"

B. Bear almost agreed—until he realized that his backpack was gone! Looking around, he saw all his school supplies floating down the stream, with the current.

"My stuff!" he cried.

"Come back!" he yelled to the forest
creatures taking his school supplies.
But it was no use.

"Come on, B. Bear," Lolly said gently.
"It's time to go to school."

"No! I needed those!" cried B. Bear. Tears
rolled down his furry cheeks.

"It'll be okay," she told him. "You can
borrow my pencil."

When they finally made it to school, B. Bear was still upset. "I don't have anything I need for school," he whimpered.

Lolly grabbed his hand and smiled.

Just then, B. Bear realized he had

the only thing he truly needed:

A friend!